Skyboy

and other stupendous science stories

Jonathan Emmett ■ **Simon Bartram,
Kevin Hopgood, Alex Paterson
and Yannick Robert**

Contents

OXFORD
UNIVERSITY PRESS

D0264278

Brought to You By ThinkRight

By Jonathan Emmett
Illustrated by Simon Bartram

Class 6C were having their weekly *brain-training* session. The children were queuing up in an orderly line outside the training room. The door opened and an electronic throbbing sound was heard as four children came out and another four shuffled silently into the room.

All of the children in Year 5 and 6 were being brain-trained – except George. George was back in the classroom with Miss Roberts, the teaching assistant.

A letter had gone home last term explaining what brain-training was and why the school was going to use it. The letter had said:

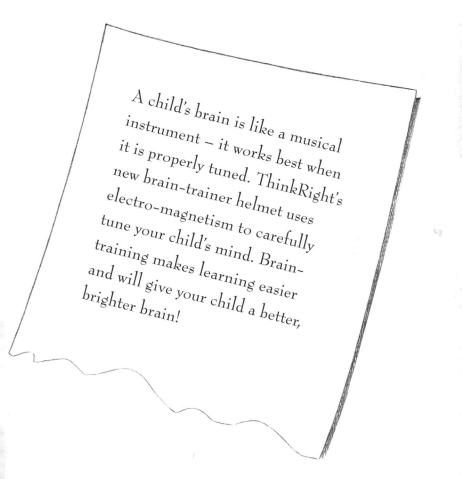

A child's brain is like a musical instrument – it works best when it is properly tuned. ThinkRight's new brain-trainer helmet uses electro-magnetism to carefully tune your child's mind. Brain-training makes learning easier and will give your child a better, brighter brain!

George's dad had frowned when he'd read the letter. "I don't like the idea of a machine changing the way you think," he'd explained to George. "I like you just as you are – even if you are a cheeky monkey!"

As the weeks went by, the brain-trained children started doing a lot better in lessons. So other parents, who had been unsure at first, had changed their minds. They had agreed to have their children brain-trained too. Now George's dad was the only parent who still hadn't agreed and George felt left out.

George finished the worksheet he'd been set and handed it to Miss Roberts.

"What shall I do now?" he asked.

"You can play quietly until break-time," said Miss Roberts. "It's only five minutes."

George went back to his desk. He took a *Collectaball* toy out of his bag. The Collectaball belonged to George's friend Rajesh. He woke up the toy by rolling it across the table. A pair of large yellow eyes lit up and the toy made an electronic purring noise.

Collectaballs were the latest craze. All the children were collecting them – but George couldn't understand why. They were just little ball-shaped creatures that made noises. That was it. They were no fun to play with and they broke apart if you threw them like normal balls. They were really expensive too! This one was called *Adoraball* and it was covered in pink fur.

George hadn't wanted to borrow the toy from Rajesh but Rajesh had gone on and on about it. In the end, George had taken it just to shut him up. Rajesh had been acting a bit weird recently. In fact, so had all of George's friends, ever since they'd started collecting the Collectaballs. All they seemed to want to do was play with them or talk about them.

"I'm Adoraball!" said the toy as it rolled against George's hand.

"No you're not," sighed George, as the bell rang for break. "You're just stupid and expensive and I can't understand why everyone thinks you're so cool."

On his way out to the playground, George passed the training room. The door was open to the empty room, which was unusual. George was curious to see what the brain-trainer helmets looked like, so he slipped inside.

The large silver helmets were fixed to stands above a row of black leather chairs. They reminded George of the big hair-dryers in his granny's hairdresser's. Bundles of cables led from the helmets and into the back of a computer. The computer's screensaver showed a brain-shaped logo with the word 'ThinkRight' across it.

George peered up into one of the helmets. The inside was covered with little pieces of smooth shiny metal. It seemed to shimmer as George looked at it.

Just as he reached out to touch the strange metal, he heard someone talking in the corridor outside.

Peeking out of the door, he spotted the head-teacher, Mrs Grayling. She was walking towards the training room. She was with a man and a woman who George didn't recognize. Both strangers were dressed in sleek, expensive-looking business suits. They looked out of place in the slightly shabby school.

George knew he wasn't meant to be in the room, so he looked for somewhere to hide.

"I must say, Miss Mesmer, the brain-training is working remarkably well," said Mrs Grayling, as she entered the room. "We've just tested the children and they're all getting much higher scores in every subject. Maths, English, History – the lot! They seem much better behaved, too. I can't believe that the school doesn't have to pay you anything for it."

"Don't worry about that," said Cordelia Mesmer smoothly. "ThinkRight knows that children are the future. We're always happy to help schools like yours. Now, Victor and I just need to upgrade the helmets' software for you, then we'll be on our way."

"Right you are," said Mrs Grayling. "Or should I say *ThinkRight* you are! I'll leave you to it. I'll be in my office if you need anything."

The only place to hide in the training room was next to the computer desk. Squatting down, trying to make himself as small as possible, George spotted the Collectaball's electronic eyes blinking up at him from inside his bag. He must have woken the toy accidentally in his hurry to hide. If the Collectaball started making its stupid noises, he was bound to be discovered. George carefully slid off the battery cover to take out the batteries.

Victor sat at the desk beside George. He began to type on the computer keyboard. Anxious not to be discovered, George tried to ease the batteries out of the Collectaball's side.

"Which one is it? The Adoraball?" asked Victor.

George froze. Victor must have spotted him.

"No, the Adoraball was last month," said Cordelia. "We want them to start buying the *Invinciball* this month. It's meant to look like a superhero. Not that it matters what it looks like."

"Yeah, the kids will buy whatever this thing tells them to!" chuckled Victor.

George relaxed a little. He hadn't been discovered after all. But what did Victor mean?

The Collectaball's eyes began to blink. George knew that, any moment now, it would start purring. He jammed his thumbnail into the toy and managed to pry out the batteries at last.

He was about to slip the toy back into his bag when something caught his eye. It was a tiny label that had been hidden beneath the batteries. It read: *Manufactured by ThinkRight Ltd.*

ThinkRight – that was the same company that made the brain-trainer helmets. It was also the same company that Cordelia and Victor worked for! Suddenly, it all made sense. The helmets didn't just make children easier to teach; they made them buy Collectaballs as well. That was the real reason the company let the school use the helmets for free. To make millions selling overpriced toys.

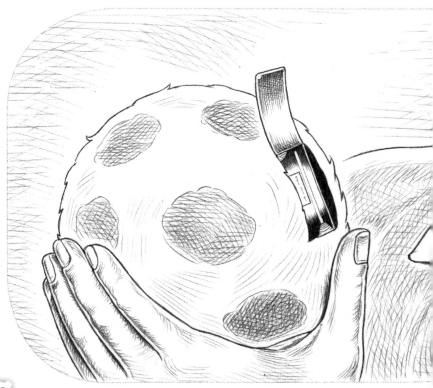

George realized that he needed to tell Mrs Grayling. If she knew what ThinkRight were really up to, she could put a stop to it. There must be schools all over the country using the brain-training helmets! That meant hundreds of thousands of children were being brainwashed by ThinkRight. At present, children were only buying Collectaballs, but they could be made to buy chocolate bars, fizzy drinks, clothing, music ... anything that ThinkRight wanted to sell.

By the time George realized that his hands were shaking, it was too late. The Adoraball slipped from his fingers and rolled out across the floor.

George heard Victor say, "Where did that come from?" Then Miss Mesmer was staring right at him.

"Well, look what we have here!" she said, with a sinister smile...

George's dad couldn't help noticing that his son didn't seem to be his usual cheeky self when he picked George up from school later that day.

"Did something happen at school today?" Dad asked, as they walked home. "Something you want to tell me about?"

"No, thank you," said George. "I'm fine."

"OK," said Dad, although he still felt that something wasn't quite right.

"We need to pop into the supermarket on the way home. Is there anything you want while we're there?" asked his dad.

Suddenly, George's face lit up.

"There is something," he said. "Please, can I have one of those Collectaballs? There's a new one called Invinciball – it looks just like a superhero!"

By Jonathan Emmett
Illustrated by Kevin Hopgood

Later ...

What do you want?

The Greatest Scientist of All Time

Presented to Horatio Hawkins

By Jonathan Emmett
Illustrated by Alex Paterson

Setting the scene

PROFESSOR HORATIO HAWKINS is in his 60s. He is a great professor who has won many awards but has a high opinion of himself.

SIMON is Horatio's nine-year-old grandson. He shares his grandfather's intelligence but has more common sense.

FENELLA FINESTEIN is in her 40s. She is a brilliant scientist from the future who has invented time travel.

The setting: The play is set in Horatio's lab. It is jam-packed with awards and expensive scientific equipment. Half-finished experiments litter the benches. It is late in the evening, after Horatio has received his latest award.

Night-time. Inside a science laboratory.
PROFESSOR HORATIO HAWKINS and his
grandson SIMON enter. SIMON is carrying a
gold trophy.

HORATIO: Well, Simon, that was a splendid
evening. It's always nice to pick
up an award. But now I must get
on with my work.

SIMON: *(sniffing with a cold)* Of course,
Grandpa. Where would you like
me to put this trophy?

HORATIO: Oh, just put it with all the others
- *(laughs)* if you can find some
space!

SIMON puts the trophy on a set of shelves
crammed with other trophies and awards.

HORATIO: Look at them all. Awards for
my work in biology, chemistry,
physics, astronomy ... every area
of science you could imagine.
What should I turn my brilliant
mind to next?

SIMON: *(blows nose on hanky)* Why don't you find a cure for the common cold?

HORATIO: *(shaking his head)* The common cold! Really, Simon, I'm Horatio Hawkins - the greatest scientist of all time. Do you seriously think I should waste my time on something as simple as the common cold? No, it needs to be something important, something that could change the course of history. *(thinks for a moment)* I know! I shall invent TIME TRAVEL!

The laboratory lights flicker on and off and there is an electronic zapping sound. When the lights come on again, PROFESSOR FENELLA FINESTEIN has mysteriously appeared in the middle of the laboratory.

FENELLA: *(fiddling with an electronic bracelet she's wearing)* Excellent! It works! I knew it would.

HORATIO: *(astonished)* Who are you? How did you get into my laboratory?

FENELLA: I'm Professor Fenella Finestein and I got here using this *(shows electronic bracelet),* my latest invention. I call it the ChronoTrekker – it allows me to travel through time.

SIMON: You're from the future! Where – I mean when?

FENELLA: The year 3215. You must be Simon and this must be your grandfather, Professor Hawkins. What an old-fashioned laboratory *(looking around).* It's amazing to think that this is how scientists actually used to work.

HORATIO: 'Old-fashioned'! This is the most up-to-date laboratory on the planet!

FENELLA: Of course it is. I didn't mean to upset you. I realize that all this junk, ... erm ... I mean equipment, must seem very impressive to a primitive mind like yours.

HORATIO: 'Primitive'! How dare you! Why I'm the greatest scientist of all time!

FENELLA: *(laughing) The greatest scientist of all time?* You can't be serious? Oh dear, I rather think you are. Well, I hate to break it to you but in my time hardly anyone's heard of you. No, *the greatest scientist of all time* – that would have to be me!

Horatio, who is not used to being talked down to, is speechless with anger. His mouth moves but no sound comes out. He clenches and unclenches his fists.

SIMON: So why are you here?

FENELLA: Well, although I invented the ChronoTrekker, I did have to use a rather brilliant idea that your grandfather here is supposed to have dreamt up. It's called Hawkins' Theory of Time Travel.

SIMON: So Grandpa does invent time travel!

FENELLA: Hardly, my dear. It's nearly all my work – Hawkins' theory is just a teeny bit of it.

SIMON: But if it's called *Hawkins'* theory then Grandpa must discover it!

FENELLA: Ah, but the thing is, I don't think he does discover it. You see, I got the theory from this notebook that I found in the museum. *(takes a bound notebook out of her pocket)*

HORATIO: *(stops looking angry and looks surprised)* That looks like MY notebook! *(taking an identical notebook out of his pocket)*

FENELLA: That's because it *is* your notebook – but this one's from the future. It's got the Theory of Time Travel written in it, look. *(Passing the book to HORATIO)*

HORATIO: Amazing! This is definitely my notebook. *(looking through the book's pages)* 'Theory of Time Travel' *(reads silently for a moment)* ... OH, I say! This really is extraordinarily clever. *(smiles to himself)*

FENELLA: Well that's the thing. It's far cleverer than any of your other discoveries. There's no way a mind as simple as yours could have come up with it.

HORATIO is struck speechless with anger.

FENELLA: Which got me wondering. If you're not smart enough to discover the theory, then someone must have given it to you. But who could have come up with such a brilliant theory? And then I realized that once I got the ChronoTrekker working, I could travel back in time and give you the theory myself. So here I am!

HORATIO: I don't need you to give it to me! I'm sure I'll work it out on my own without any help from you. You can go straight back to wherever – I mean *whenever* you came from.

FENELLA: Oh dear. I wasn't expecting you to be clever but I didn't think you'd be this moronic!

HORATIO: *(shouting)* MORONIC! MORONIC!

FENELLA: *(slowly, as if talking to a child)* Yes. It's another word for stupid.

HORATIO: *(shouting)* I KNOW WHAT IT MEANS!

SIMON: *(stepping between them)* WAIT A MINUTE! I've just realized something. If Professor Finestein knows the theory because she found it in this notebook ...

HORATIO and FENELLA: *(impatiently)* Yes!

SIMON: ... and she travels back from the future and gives the notebook to Grandpa, so that he can discover it ...

FENELLA: Or claim to have discovered it!

SIMON: ... then who actually came up with this theory? Who actually wrote it in the book?

HORATIO: Isn't it obvious? It must have been me because ... *(scratches head and thinks for a moment)* ... oh, I don't know!

FENELLA: I can explain it. It must have been me because ... *(rubs chin and thinks)* ... oh, I don't know either! But the fact is, everyone in the future thinks you discovered it, even though I just gave it to you.

SIMON: *(thoughtfully)* I don't think either of you came up with the theory. It's as if the words in the notebook just exist without anyone actually writing them down. But that's impossible – isn't it?

FENELLA: *(impatiently)* Well, whoever *really* came up with the theory, your numbskull grandpa has to pretend it was him. Because without Hawkins' Theory, I could not have invented the ChronoTrekker and I would not be here right now.

HORATIO: *(angrily)* Well I have to say,
           the idea of you not being *here*
           sounds extremely appealing – to a
           'numbskull' like me.

*HORATIO rips a couple of pages from the
notebook, stuffs them into his mouth and
chews them.*

SIMON: What are you doing Grandpa?

HORATIO: *(chewing the paper)* Getting rid
           ... *(chews)* ... of this dreadful ...
           (chews) ... theory. I've decided
           that ... *(chews)* ... time travel may
           not be ... *(chews)* ... such a good
           invention after all.

FENELLA: *(shocked)* But Hawkins, if you
           destroy that ...

HORATIO: *(swallows)* There we go – all gone!

The laboratory lights flicker on and off. All three characters move quickly backwards, as if the scene they've just acted is a video recording that is being rewound rapidly. Speeded-up backwards speech is heard at the same time and then an electronic zapping sound.

When the lights come on again, FENELLA has disappeared and HORATIO and SIMON are back at the beginning of the play.

SIMON puts the trophy on a set of shelves crammed with other trophies and awards.

HORATIO: Look at them all. Awards for my work in biology, chemistry, physics, astronomy … every area of science you could imagine. What should I turn my brilliant mind to next?

SIMON: *(blows nose on hanky)* Why don't you find a cure for the common cold?

HORATIO: *(looks as if he is about to shake his head as he did the first time, but then pauses, before nodding enthusiastically)* The common cold! What a brilliant suggestion. You know, Simon, you have the makings of an excellent scientist. Keep thinking like that and you could be *the greatest scientist of all time!*

My Cousin is a Cucumber

By Jonathan Emmett
Illustrated by Yannick Robert

My cousin is a cucumber!
Your cousin is one too!
We've got cousins in the greenhouse
and cousins in the zoo.

You see, a man called Darwin,
a scientist of course,
discovered every living thing
had sprung from just one source:
an itsy-bitsy blob of life,
four billion years ago,
the ancestor of everything,
of all the life we know!

So everything's related
in one great family tree,
every mouse and mushroom,
every flower and flea.
And, animal or vegetable,
immense or very small.
A lot of our genetic code
is common to us all.

So if a fly comes buzzing by,
invite it in for tea!
Remember, it's your cousin
and we're ONE BIG FAMILY!

Discover the hidden worlds of science in *Under the Microscope*.

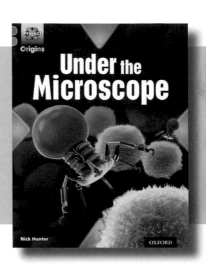

Read all about the work of the some of the world's best scientists and find out how they shocked the world in *Science Shocks!*

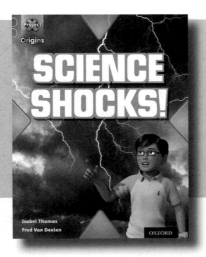